APOCALYP...

CW00495658

COMPLETE RECORD...
ILLUSTRATED

ANDREW SPARKE

Essential Discographies No.166

APS PUBLICATIONS

APS Books,
The Stables, Field Lane
Aberford, West Yorkshire,
LS25 3AE

APS Books is a subsidiary of the APS Publications imprint

www.andrewsparke.com

Cover photograph courtesy of Stock Ruiz & www.shutterstock.com
Frontispiece photograph courtesy of Olga Popova & www.shutterstock.com

APOCALYPTICA

Unique is the only word for a band that choose to play heavy metal on cellos and one that's Finnish to boot, Finland being a country almost completely under-represented in the international rock music scene - with the exception of a short period in the early 1970s when progressive rock held sway long enough to notice WIGWAM, the solo albums of their bassist PEKKA POHJOLA, the band TASAVALLAN PRESIDENTTI and their guitarist JUKKA TOLENEN.

Apocalyptica formed in Helsinki in 1993 by the classically trained cellist, Eicca Toppinen, and three of his fellow students at the Sibelius Academy. Unsurprisingly for much of the band's existence they have been an instrumental quartet which started out playing the music of METALLICA on their cellos. Subsequently from 2000 they have used guest vocalists on occasion but the core of their work has remained a brand of exciting metal that manages without guitar and bass, instruments previously thought vital to their chosen musical form.

Alongside their own compositions they have continued to record cover versions of songs by other metal bands including SEPULTERA and PANTERA (as well as recording 'Helden', the German version of 'Heroes' by DAVID BOWIE) and have performed with RAMMSTEIN and also with METALLICA in celebration of their 30th Anniversary on 5th December 2011.

For a project which might have seemed likely to be short-lived when they started, Apocalyptica has proved a long-lived success, with nine studio albums under their belts to date and all being well, the band will celebrate their own 30th anniversary in 2023.

APOCALYPTICA MUSICIANS

EICCA TOPPINEN *(cello) (1993–present)*
PAAVO LÖTJÖNEN *(cello) (1993–present)*
PERTTU KIVILAAKSO *(cello, programming) (1995, 1999–present)*
MIKKO SIRÉN *(drums & percussion, programming) (2003-present)*
MAX LILJA *(cello) (1993–2002)*
ANTERO MANNINEN *(cello) (1993–1999) (live/touring member: 2002–*
2009, 2017–2018)
TIPE JOHNSON *(vocals) (touring member: 2009–2012, 2019)*
FRANKY PEREZ *(vocals) (touring member: 2014–2016, 2022-present)*
LAURI KANKKUNEN *(cello) (touring member: 2019)*

Apocalyptica at Hellfest2017 courtesy of Selby May

PLAYS METALLICA BY FOUR CELLOS

(1996 Mercury)

Enter Sandman
Master of Puppets
Harvester of Sorrow
The Unforgiven
Sad But True
Creeping Death
Wherever I May Roam
Welcome Home (Sanitarium)

INQUISITION SYMPHONY

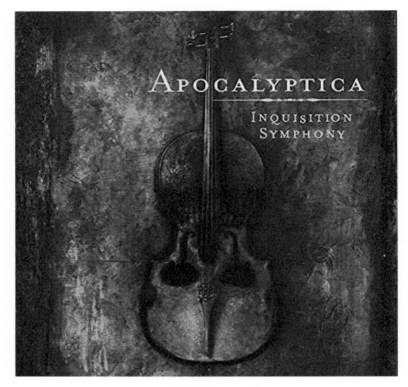

(1998 Mercury)

Harmageddon
From Out of Nowhere
For Whom the Bell Tolls
Nothing Else Matters
Refuse/Resist
M.B.
Inquisition Symphony
Fade to Black
Domination
Toreador
One

CULT

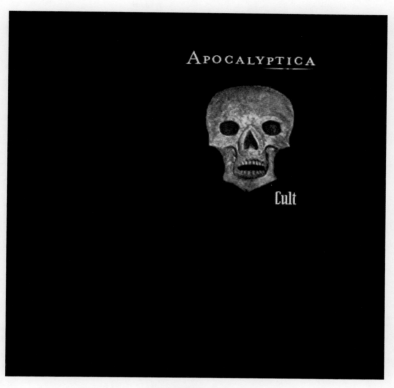

(2000 Mercury)

Path	Hope
Struggle	Kaamos
Romance	Coma *(live)*
Pray!	Hall of the Mountain King
In Memoriam	Until It Sleeps
Hyperventilation	Fight Fire With Fire
Beyond Time	

Path, Volume 2 (feat. Sandra Nasic)
Hope, Volume 2 (feat. Matthias Sayer)
Harmageddon (live in Munich)
Nothing Else Matters (live in Munich)
Inquisition Symphony (live in Munich)

WAGNER RELOADED – LIVE IN LEIPZIG

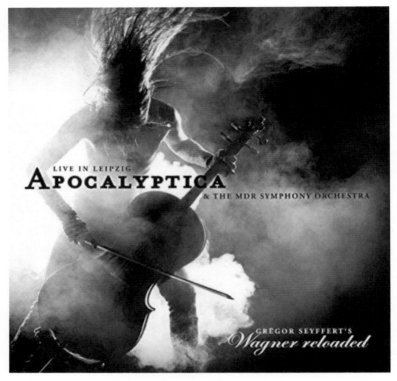

(2002 BMG)

Signal
Genesis
Fight Against Monsters
Stormy Wagner
Flying Dutchman
Lullaby
Bubbles
Path In Life
Creation Of Notes
Running Love
Birth Pain
Ludwig – Wonderland
Ludwig – Requiem
Destruction

REFLECTIONS

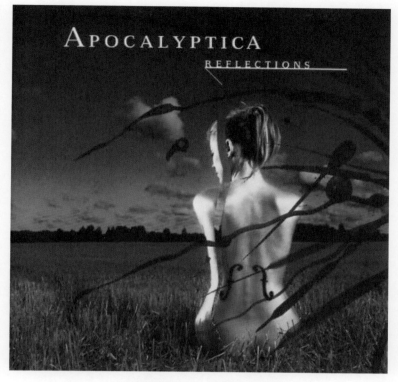

(2003 Island/Universal)

Prologue (Apprehension)
No Education
Faraway
Somewhere Around Nothing
Drive
Cohkka
Conclusion
Resurrection
Heat
Cortége

Pandemonium
Toreador II
Epilogue (Relief)
Seemann – with Nina Hagen
Faraway, Volume 2 (feat. Linda) (extended version)

Delusion
Perdition
Leave Me Alone

Faraway (live at Rock am Ring)
Enter Sandman (live at Rock am Ring)
Inquisition Symphony (live at Rock am Ring)
Nothing Else Matters (live)
Somewhere Around Nothing (live)
Somewhere Around Nothing (video)
Faraway (feat. Linda) (video)
Seemann (feat. Nina Hagen) (video)
Making of Faraway (feat. Linda)
Making of Reflections
Making of Seemann with Nina Hagen

(2014 Harmageddon)

APOCALYPTICA

(2005 Vertigo/Universal)

Life Burns!
Quutamo
Distraction
Bittersweet
Misconstruction
Fisheye
Farewell
Fatal Error
Betrayal/Forgiveness
Ruska
Deathzone / En Vie
En Vie
How Far
Wie Weit
Bittersweet (Video)

WORLDS COLLIDE

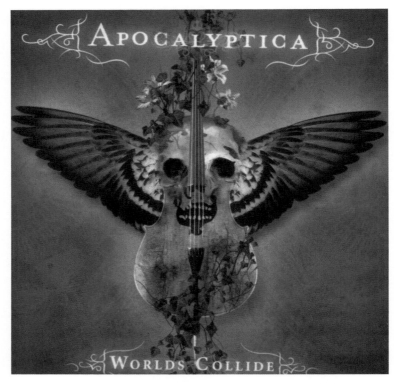

(2007 Sony BMG)

Worlds Collide
Grace
I'm Not Jesus
Ion
Helden
Stroke
Last Hope
I Don't Care
Burn
S.O.S. (Anything but Love)
Peace
Ural
Dreamer
Lies

CD comes with DVD

7ᵀᴴ SYMPHONY

(2010 Sony Music)

At the Gates of Manala
End of Me
Not Strong Enough
2010
Through Paris in a Sportscar
Beautiful
Broken Pieces
On the Rooftop with Quasimodo
Bring Them to Light
Sacra
Rage of Poseidon
The Shadow of Venus
Spiral Architect – Black Sabbath
Path (Acoustic Version)
The Unforgiven (Acoustic Version)

SHADOWMAKER

(2015 Eleven Seven Music)

I-III-V Seed of Chaos
Cold Blood
Shadowmaker
Slow Burn
Hole in My Soul
House of Chains
Riot Lights
Sea Song (You Waded Out)
Till Death Do Us Part
Dead Man's Eyes

CELL-O

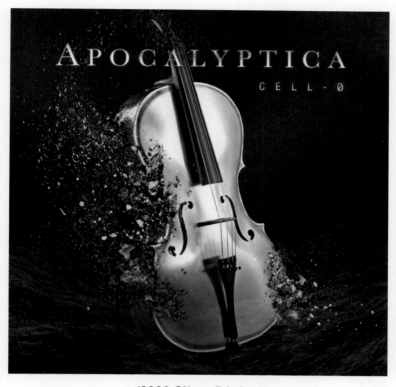

(2020 Silver Lining)

Ashes of the Modern World
Cell-0
Rise
En Route to Mayhem
Call My Name
Fire & Ice
Scream for the Silent
Catharsis
Beyond the Stars

COMPILATIONS

THE BEST OF APOCALYPTICA

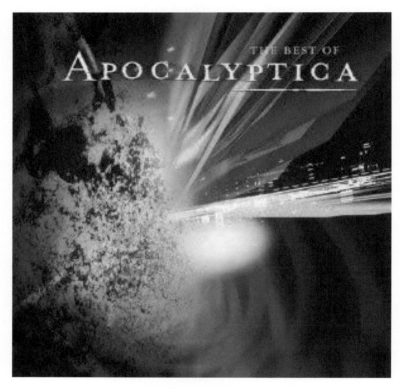

(2002 Universal)

Driven
Hope
Enter Sandman
Nothing Else Matters
Pray!
Path
The Unforgiven
Refuse/Resist
Kaamos
Inquisition Symphony
Romance
Harmageddon
Hall of the Mountain King

AMPLIFIED
A DECADE OF REINVENTING THE CELLO

(2006 20-20 Records)

Enter Sandman	Kaamos
Harmageddon	Deathzone
Nothing Else Matters	Angel of Death
Refuse/Resist	Repressed
Somewhere Around Nothing	Path Vol. 2
Betrayal	Bittersweet
Farewell	Hope Vol. 2
Master of Puppets	En Vie
Hall of the Mountain King	Faraway Vol. 2
One	Life Burns
Heat	Seemann
Cohkka	

Paavo Lötjönen and Perttu Kivilaakso 2018 courtesy of Stefan Bottmann

Eicca Toppinen and Antero Mannine 2018 courtesy of Stefan Bottmann

SINGLES

Enter Sandman *(1996)*
O Holy Night/Little Drummer Boy *(1996)*
The Unforgiven *(1996)*

Harmageddon/From Out Of Nowhere/Enter Sandman *(live)*/The
Unforgiven *(live) (1998)*
The Path Vol.1&2 (featuring Sandra Nasić) (2000)
Hope Vol.2 (featuring Matthias Sayer) (2002)

Faraway Vol.2 (featuring Linda Sundblad) (2003)
Seemann (featuring Nina Hagen) (2003)
Somewhere Around Nothing (2003)

Bittersweet (featuring Ville Valo & Lauri Ylönen) (2005)
Wie Weit/How Far/En Vie (featuring Marta Jandova & Manu) (2005)
Life Burns (featuring Lauri Ylönen) (2005)

Repressed (featuring Matt Tuck & Max Cavalera) (2006)
I'm Not Jesus (featuring Corey Taylor) (2007)
S.O.S. (Anything but Love) (featuring Cristina Scabbia) (2008)

I Don't Care (featuring Adam Gontier) (2008)
End Of Me (featuring Gavin Rossdale) (2010)
Broken Pieces (featuring Lacey Mosley) (2010)

Not Strong Enough (featuring Brent Smith) (2010)
Not Strong Enough (featuring Doug Robb) (2011)
Shadowmaker (2014)
Slow Burn (2015)
Cold Blood (2015)
Sin In Justice (with Vamps) (2015)

Me melkein kuoltiin (featuring Sanni & Tippa) (2019)
Fields Of Verdun (2019)
Live Or Die (2020)

White Room (featuring Jacoby Shaddix) (2021)
Peltirumpu (2022)

DVDS

Printed in Great Britain
by Amazon

16332576R00016